Redi Fox

Dave and Pat Sargent are longtime residents of Prairie Grove, Arkansas. Dave, a fourth-generation dairy farmer, began writing in early December 1990, and Pat, a former teacher, began writing shortly after. They enjoy the outdoors and have a real love for animals.

Redi Fox

By

Dave and Pat Sargent

Illustrated by
Jean Lirley Huff

Ozark Publishing, Inc.
P.O. Box 228
Prairie Grove, AR 72753

iii

Library of Congress cataloging-in-publication data

Sargent, Dave, 1941--
      Redi Fox / Dave and Pat Sargent ; illustrated by
Jean Huff.
            p. cm. — (Animal pride series ; 3)
      Summary: A red fox makes friends with a
young girl and comes to her rescue when   she almost
steps on a copperhead snake. Includes facts about the
physical   characteristics, behavior, habitat, and
predators of the wolf.
      ISBN 1-56763-010-3. — ISBN 1-56763-085-5
(alk. paper)
      1. Red fox—Juvenile fiction. [1. Red fox—
Fiction. 2. Foxes—Fiction.] I. Sargent,   Pat, 1936-
. II. Huff, Jean, ill. III. Title. IV. Series: Sargent,
Dave, 1941-   animal pride   series ; 3.
            PZ10.3.S243Re   1996
            [Fic]—dc20
            96-1496
            CIP
            AC

Printed in the United States of America

Inspired by

our granddaughter, April Michon. When April was two years old, she told us a story, over and over, about a little red fox who chased her.

Dedicated to

the sweetest little girl in the world, April Michon Sargent Kassel.

Foreword

Redi, a sly and cunning little red fox, makes friends with Farmer John's daughter. Redi puts his life on the line one day, when April almost steps on a copperhead snake.

Contents

One   Redi Fox   1

Two   The Copperhead Snake   9

Three   Redi The Hero   17

Four   Fox Facts   25

Redi Fox

If you would like to have the authors of the Animal Pride Series visit your school, free of charge, call 1-800-321-5671 or 1-800-960-3876.

One

Redi Fox

Redi Fox lived in a den with his two brothers, two sisters, and his mama and papa, short distance from Farmer John's house.

Mama Fox told her young pups, "All of you leave Farmer John's chickens alone. He doesn't care if we live nearby as long as we don't bother his chickens."

Redi was a sly little red fox who loved to play all the time. He also liked to explore. When his mama was gone to look for food, all the fox pups, except Redi, would stay in the den. Redi was usually outside looking around.

Redi Fox spent much of his time on top of a small hill near the den watching Farmer John coming and going. He always wondered what Farmer John was doing.

Farmer John had a daughter named April, and April was a lot like Redi. She was often outside playing in the yard. Because she was five years old, she was supposed to stay in sight of the house when she played outside, but sometimes, young April wandered off into the fields looking at all the wildflowers.

One day when April was out picking wildflowers to give to her mother, she came to the small hill where Redi Fox always played. She didn't know it, but Redi was lying on top of the hill watch ing her every move.

April looked at the hill and thought, "I think I'll climb this little hill and see if there are any pretty flowers on top of it."

4

When April started up the small hill, Redi Fox sat up and barked at her. He was trying to scare her away.

When April saw Redi, she said, "Oh, what a pretty little red fox. He would be fun to play with."

Redi wasn't sure about April, and said to himself, "I think I'll chase that little girl off my hill.

When April saw Redi Fox start down the hill toward her, she turned around and ran. Redi stopped and barked at her. Now, when Redi Fox began barking, April thought he wanted to play, so she began chasing him.

Redi took off around the hill with April right behind him. They chased each other back and forth for a long time.

When April heard her mother calling, she stopped playing and said, "I have to go now, little fox, but I'll be back tomorrow, and we can play some more."

As April walked toward the big farmhouse, Redi Fox took his place on top of the small hill and watched her. He thought to himself, "Boy, that sure was a lot of fun. I hope that little girl comes back again soon."

It wasn't long until Redi's mama came home. She had brought the pups some food. She spotted Redi on top of the hill and asked, "What are you doing, Redi?"

"I'm watching Farmer John's daughter," Redi replied.

Mama Fox smiled at Redi and then called, "You pups come eat."

The next day, Mama Fox left to search for food. It was a full-time job feeding her five growing pups. Papa Fox had gone on a hunting trip and wouldn't be back for several days. Feeding and caring for the young pups was Mama Fox's job now.

Two

The Copperhead Snake

While Mama Fox was gone, Redi lay on top of the small hill watching for April. Finally, he saw her coming out the front door.

Redi waited anxiously as April ran through the tall grass toward the small hill. As she neared the top of the hill, Redi Fox took off. The chase was on.

They chased each other around the hill for a long time until they heard April's mother calling. April said, "I have to go now, little fox, but I'll be back soon."

April ran home, so Redi stayed on top of the small hill all alone. When April got to the front door, she turned and waved at Redi. He saw her wave, and it made him feel good inside. He liked April.

Days passed before Redi saw April again. He began to think that she was never coming back to play. But one day she came skipping across the field toward Redi's hill.

Farmer John had cut the grass so it was very short now. He had cut the grass so he would have hay to feed to his milk cows during the coming winter.

The grass on the small hill was still quite tall. Farmer John had not cut it because he was afraid his mowing machine and hay baler would turn over.

As April neared the top of the hill, Redi Fox jumped up and began wagging his tail. He sure was glad to see her. They ran and played for a long time. Suddenly, Redi stopped. He sensed danger nearby.

April looked at Redi and asked, "What's wrong, little fox?" She started walking toward Redi, then stopped and looked down. Right in front of her feet was a copperhead snake. The snake was coiled up, ready to strike!

When April realized that she had almost stepped on the snake, she screamed!

Redi jumped on the copperhead snake and grabbed it with his sharp teeth. He shook the snake hard, by slinging his head back and forth.

Molly, April's mother, had heard her scream and started running across the field toward the hill. When she got close enough, she saw Redi Fox fighting the copperhead.

Molly yelled, "April!" April ran to meet her mother. Redi yelped! The snake had bitten him.

Redi Fox let out another yelp. The snake had bitten him again. He let the snake go and headed for his den.

Redi had been bitten on the face and on the front foot. He was in great pain. He had saved April's life, but now, he would probably die.

When Redi's mother got home, she found Redi asleep. She noticed that his head was swollen real big and his front leg was swollen, also.

Mama Fox tried to wake Redi, but she couldn't. He wouldn't wake up. She knew he had been bitten by a poisonous snake of some kind.

Mama Fox said, "I know that Redi is smart enough to stay away from snakes. I can't understand why he would bother one."

She found the other cubs and asked, "Do you cubs know what happened to Redi?"

They replied, "No, Mama, we don't know what happened to him. We were in the den when we heard Farmer John's daughter scream.

Then we heard Redi yelp two times. Is Redi going to be all right, Mama? Or will he die?"

"I don't know," Mama Fox said I certainly hope he doesn't die."

Mama Fox didn't tell the pups, but she was very afraid that Redi would die. She thought to herself, "Redi is much too young to survive a bite from a poisonous snake."

Three

Redi The Hero

April's mother, knew that the little red fox had saved April's life. When Farmer John came in from the field, Molly explained to him what had happened. She told him about the copperhead snake, and how the little fox had saved their daughter.

Farmer John said, "I'm glad the foxes have made their home on our farm. They can live here as long as they please."

The next day, April took a bowl of warm milk and set it on the small hill for Redi. She called and called.

When Redi didn't come, she left the bowl of milk on top of the hill and went home.

Early the next day, April took another small bowl of warm milk to the top of the hill. She found that the bowl she had left the day before hadn't been touched. She poured out the old milk and took the empty bowl home.

On the third morning after Redi had been bitten by the copperhead snake, April took a small jar of warm milk to the little red fox. The bowl of milk from the day before was still sitting there. It had not been touched. She poured it out and filled the bowl with fresh milk. She called and called, but there was no sign of Redi. She sighed and said, "I wonder if the little red fox will ever come out of the den? I wonder if he is still alive." She was very sad as she went down the hill to her home.

April knew that she must not give up hope yet. Early the next morning, she took another jar of warm milk to the top of the hill.

Day after day, April did this. And finally, one morning, when she got to the top of the hill, she found an empty bowl. "Did the little red fox drink the milk, or did something else drink it?" April wondered.

She poured fresh warm milk into the bowl and called, "Come on, little fox. Come drink your milk." April called again and again. Then, just as she turned to go home, she heard a very low whining sound. Turning around, April saw Redi creeping from the den.

Painfully, Redi Fox half-walked and half-crawled to the bowl of warm milk and started drinking.

April reached out and rubbed Redi Fox on the head. She said, "You saved my life, little red fox. I'm going to bring you warm milk and something good to eat every day until you are well. My daddy says that you can live here on our farm as long as you want."

Every day, without fail, April took warm milk to Redi. Sometimes she carried biscuits and gravy to him. And each day, when Redi had finished eating, she would pet him. They became close friends.

After several days, April looked out the window and saw Redi sitting on top of the hill waiting for her to bring him his lunch. This made her happy to have a good friend like Redi.

Redi was slowly getting his strength back and began playing with April more every day. When she played with him, she could hear the other young foxes in the den, but they would never come out when she was around.

One day, Farmer John decided to go with April to feed the little fox. When Redi Fox saw Farmer John coming, he ran and hid in the den and wouldn't come out.

April called, "Come out, little fox. I want you to meet my daddy." But Redi would not come out of the den.

After several minutes had past, Farmer John said, "It looks like the little red fox is not hungry today."

April said, "I saw him sitting on the hill waiting for me."

Farmer John said, "Maybe the little fox is afraid of me. I'd best go on back to the house so he will come out and eat." He walked down the hill and a few minutes later, Redi crawled out of the den and ran to the top of the hill to drink his milk.

After finishing his milk, Redi jumped up on April and licked her cheek.

April said, "I have to go home now, little fox. Why don't you come home with me?"

April walked a short distance, then looked back. Redi Fox was not following her. He would not leave the top of the hill.

April and Redi played together during the months that followed, but Redi would never leave the little hill.

April and Redi Fox became the best of friends. Even though he would never go home with April, he always barked at her when she was outside walking from the house to the barn or when she came near the hill.

Redi knew that, as long as he lived, he would have a good home, for he would always be welcome on Farmer John's place.

Four

Fox Facts

The fox is a very bushy-tailed, sharp-snouted member of the dog family. True foxes include the arctic fox, the gray fox, and the red fox. Several fox-like animals are also called foxes. Foxes and fox-like animals live throughout the world. Red foxes live in most of northern North America, Europe, and Asia. Red Foxes are the most common foxes of the northern United States and Canada. They are found in farmlands, deserts, and even in wooded areas of some suburbs.

Foxes are quick, skillful hunters. They hunt mostly at night. Unlike some animals who hibernate, foxes remain active the year around. They often roam grassy meadows to listen for the squeaks of mice. The grass conceals the mice, but if a fox sees a slight movement of blades of grass, it jumps onto the spot. Foxes some-times stand on their hind legs to get a better view in tall grass.

A fox also may lie in wait and pounce on a ground squirrel or a woodchuck as the victim leaves its burrow.

The red fox can easily catch a dodging rabbit. This fox can also creep silently toward a bird, then rush up and pounce on it.

Some people hunt the red fox because of its skill in trying to avoid capture. Many hunters seek only the excitement of the chase and do not kill the fox. The hunters use hounds to follow the scent of the fox. But the fox may double back on its trail or run into water, making its scent difficult to follow. A fox has keen hearing and an excellent sense of smell. It depends especially on these two senses in locating prey. A red fox can hear a mouse squeak over one hundred feet away. Foxes are quick to see moving objects, but they do not always notice objects that are motionless.

Some foxes, especially the red fox, and the arctic fox, have long, soft fur that is valued highly. People trap foxes for their fur and also raise the animals on fur farms. Most red foxes have bright rusty-red or red-orange fur with whitish fur on the belly. They have blackish legs and a white tip on the tail.

Not all red foxes have red coats. Some, called silver foxes, have coats of black fur tipped with white. Silver foxes may appear blackish gray, or frosty silver, depending on the length of the white tips. Silver foxes with black fur are called black foxes.

Other red foxes, called cross foxes, have rusty-red coats with a large black cross at the shoulders. The cross extends down the middle of the back. Silver foxes, cross foxes, and typical red foxes may be born at the same time to the same parents.

Most foxes are about the same size. Gray foxes and red foxes grow from twenty-three to twenty-seven inches long. The tail measures an additional fourteen to sixteen inches. Most of these foxes weigh from eight to eleven pounds.

Most species of foxes resemble small, slender dogs. Foxes have a bushy tail. Most carry their tails straight backward when they are running. The tail droops when the animal walks. A fox may sleep with its tail over its nose and front paws.

Many foxes have a scent gland on the tail. Scent from this gland gives foxes a distinctive odor. These animals also have large, pointed ears and a long, sharp snout.

A fox has five toes on each front foot, but the first toe is not completely developed. It is called a dew claw and does not reach the ground. Each hind foot has only four toes. When the animal walks or trots, its hind paws step into the tracks of the front paws.

Foxes live in family groups while the young are growing up. At other times, they live alone or in pairs. They do not form packs as wolves do. A male and a female mate in early winter. They play together and cooperate in hunting. If one of a pair of foxes is chased by an enemy, its mate may dash out of a hiding place and lead the pursuers away.

Foxes communicate with one another with growls, yelps, and short, yapping barks. A fox also makes scent stations by urinating at various spots. The scent tells foxes in the area that another fox is present.

The male fox is called a dog. The female is called a vixen, and the young is called a pup or cub. A female gives birth in late winter or early spring. The gestation period is fourty-nine to seventy-nine days, depending on the species. Red foxes have from four to nine pups at a time, and gray foxes have from three to five. Both the vixen and the dog bring their pups food and will lead enemies away from them. Foxes may live up to fourteen years.

A newborn fox weighs about four ounces and has a short muzzle and closed eyes. Its eyes open about nine days after birth.

Pups drink the mother's milk for about five weeks. Then they begin to eat some solid food and leave their den for short periods. Later, the pups wrestle with one another and pounce on insects, leaves, sticks, and their parents' tails. The adults also bring live mice for the young to pounce on. Later, the adults show the pups how to stalk prey.

The pups start to live on their own in late summer. They either separate then, or in early fall, and rejoin during the winter.

Foxes settle in dens after they mate. The den may be underground, in a cave, in a hollow log or tree, or in a pile of rocks. Some red foxes dig their own dens, but most use the burrows abandoned by such animals as woodchucks. The foxes may enlarge a burrow if necessary. An underground den may be as long as seventy-five feet and have several entrances. A main tunnel leads to several chambers that the animals use for nests and for storing food. Two pairs of red foxes may share one burrow. Gray foxes dig less than red foxes. Most gray foxes live in caves, rock piles, logs, or tree holes.

Many kinds of foxes live in dens only while raising pups. After the pups have grown old enough to hunt for themselves, the adults and the pups sleep in the open most of the time.

Foxes eat almost any animal they can catch easily, especially mice and other kinds of rodents. They also hunt birds, frogs, insects, lizards, and rabbits. Foxes also eat many kinds of fruit and the remains of dead animals. Most species hide the uneaten parts of their prey. They dig a shallow hole, drop the meat in, and spread dirt over it. A fox returns to the stored food, both to feed and, apparently, to check on it.